INSECT-EATING PLANTS

Insect-Eating Plants

L. PATRICIA KITE

7783

The Millbrook Press
Brookfield, Connecticut

Cover photograph courtesy of Fred Bavendam, Peter Arnold, Inc.

Photos courtesy of Ron West: pp. 10, 13, 14, 17 (all), 18, 20, 22, 24, 30,
32, 34, 36, 41, 50, 58; Joe Mazrimas: p. 21; Photo Researchers: pp. 26 (©
Nuridsany and Perennou), 29 (© Dr. Paul A. Zahl), 38 (© Fletcher and
Baylis), 42 (© J. H. Robinson), 46 (© Dr. Paul A. Zahl), 48 (© Jeff Lepore);
Peter Arnold, Inc.: p. 28 (© Walter H. Hodge); Lorenz Butschi: p. 44.

Library of Congress Cataloging-in-Publication Data
Kite, L. Patricia.
Insect-eating plants / by L. Patricia Kite.
p. cm.
Includes bibliographical references (p.   ) and index.
Summary: Presents the major types of carnivorous plants, including the
Venus-flytrap, pitcher plant, butterwort, sundew, and bladderwort, and
provides basic guidelines for growing carnivorous plants.
ISBN 1-56294-562-9
1. Carnivorous plants—Juvenile literature. [1. Carnivorous plants.] I. Title.
QK917.K58 1995
583′.121—dc20   94-28452 CIP AC

Published by The Millbrook Press, Inc.
2 Old New Milford Road, Brookfield, Connecticut 06804

*This book is dedicated to Joe Mazrimas,
co-founder of the International Carnivorous
Plant Society, who so delightfully whetted
my interest in carnivorous plants.*

*And also to my daughter Rachel, whose
continuous encouragement makes all the
difference.*

Pat Kite

CONTENTS

INSECT-EATING PLANTS

This sticky-leaved sundew thrives in the bog that is its home.

The word "carnivorous" means flesh-eating. Carnivorous plants, often called insect-eating plants, get some of the basic substances they need to live and grow from the flesh of insects and other small creatures.

These plants do not run after prey or grab it, the way that carnivorous animals such as lions do. Instead, they tempt insects to land on their leaves—and their leaves are insect traps.

FLESH-EATING PLANTS!

Carnivorous plants are not dangerous to people, no matter what you may have seen in movies or read in science-fiction stories. No carnivorous plant leaf is big enough to trap a person. The largest leaf is only about 3 feet (1 meter) tall. Some carnivorous plants are only the size of this "o."

In the wild, many carnivorous plants grow in bogs, swamps, and other *wetland* areas. Others grow on flat grassland. However, all carnivorous plants grow where the soil lacks some *nutrients* needed for plant growth, especially nitrogen and phosphorus. Often the soil is acid and contains *peat*.

Over thousands of years some plants adapted, or changed, to survive in this poor soil. They became carnivorous, and now they can get nutrients from insects and other tiny creatures. Can carnivorous plants grow in acid, peaty soil without this insect "food"? Most of them can. But they're not as healthy as they are when they have it.

ORDINARY PLANTS AND CARNIVOROUS PLANTS · Carnivorous plants aren't very different from ordinary green plants. An ordinary plant has roots, a stem, and leaves. The roots draw water and possible nutrients from the soil. The stem carries the water and the nutrients that are dissolved in it from the roots to the leaves.

Leaves absorb carbon dioxide from the air. At the same time, a green coloring called *chlorophyll* in the leaves helps change the energy of sunlight into chemical energy. This chemical energy then changes water, water-borne nutrients, and carbon dioxide into food the plant can use. The stem carries the food to all parts of the plant, so it can grow.

Many ordinary plants reproduce through flowers and seeds. If you look at a flower, you will see a yellow dustlike material called *pollen* in the center. Pollen from the male part of a flower (the stamen) must reach the female part of a flower (the pistil) to make fertile seeds. That's where bees and other pollen-transporting insects come in handy—they carry pollen from one flower to another.

After the seeds are fertilized, they fall to the ground or are carried to welcoming soil by insects, birds, or other animals, including people. Some of the seeds will become new plants.

Like ordinary plants, carnivorous plants have roots and stems. They have leaves containing chlorophyll, and they reproduce through flowers and seeds. But their leaves look quite a bit different from those of ordinary plants. Sometimes people think that the leaves of a carnivorous plant are its flowers because the leaves may be very colorful and beautiful.

The leaves are designed to trap insects in several different ways, and there are many nicknames for these traps: mousetrap, bear trap, steel trap, snap trap, lobster trap, suction trap, pitfall trap, pitcher trap, jug-of-water trap, flypaper trap, sticky trap. No matter what their shape, all digest, or break down, food in ways that are very like the way an animal's stomach and intestines do.

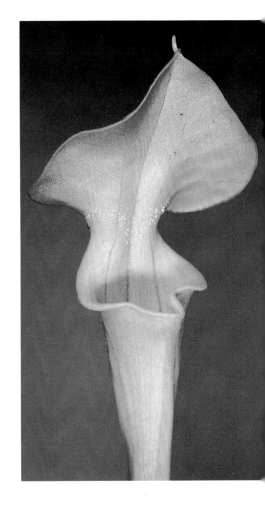

The elegant, vaselike pitcher of this yellow pitcher plant is really a special kind of leaf.

13

A single Venus flytrap has many traps.

The Venus flytrap (also called Venus's-flytrap or bear trap) can count to two. It doesn't have fingers to help it count. It has very sensitive "trigger" hairs hidden among those wicked-looking spines.

A fly or other insect wanders by, looking for a meal. Along the outer edges of Venus flytrap leaves are tiny *glands* giving off a sweet-smelling juice, or *nectar.* The Venus flytrap has pretty green outer leaves and shiny red inner leaves. It doesn't look like a dangerous plant to the hungry fly.

A SNAP TRAP: THE VENUS FLYTRAP

The closer the fly gets, the better the nectar smells. Landing on a leaf, the fly walks toward its meal. But it doesn't get very far. As soon as the fly touches two trigger hairs (or one hair twice) within twenty seconds, the two spiny leaf halves close in just a tenth of a second. That's faster than you can say "snap."

Why does it take two touches to trigger the trap? This gives the Venus flytrap a way to tell the difference between a raindrop or a wind-driven pebble and an insect meal. The plant

15

would waste too much energy if it kept closing and opening without getting nourishing food. A raindrop only falls once, and a pebble only lands once. But an insect keeps moving, letting the sensitive trigger hairs know that a meal has arrived.

When closed, Venus flytrap leaf edges make a tight trap. Now *digestive juices* flow out of leaf glands. The fly struggles for a while, then smothers. The digestive juices begin dissolving the fly's body into much smaller parts. In about ten days, the fly looks like a drop of soup. Now it is absorbed, or blotted up, by the hungry plant.

When only the *skeleton,* or tiny outside shell, of an insect remains, the trap opens. The skeleton blows away in the breeze, and the pretty Venus flytrap waits for another fly or other insect to smell its sweet nectar.

Occasionally the Venus flytrap makes a mistake and traps a piece of grass, sand, or other nonfood item. Just one day later, the leaf halves open up again, dropping the untouched nonfood item onto the ground.

Does an insect ever escape from the trap? Sometimes a snail or a big insect such as a grasshopper is strong enough to tear a leaf apart or force its way out. But that doesn't happen very often.

The scientific name of the Venus flytrap is *Dionaea muscipula,* in case you ever want to find more information in *botanical,* or plant science, books.

A mayfly lands on a Venus flytrap . . .

The trap snaps shut . . .

The trap opens several days later, revealing the remains of the digested mayfly.

This white-topped pitcher plant has developed a seed pod.

T

he bottom of a pitcher plant holds a pool of water. You wouldn't want to drink it. The water is full of dead insects that the plant is digesting and black specks that are leftover insect parts.

Some North American pitcher plants, or sarracenias, get rather large. Their pitchers, which are specially shaped leaves, can be 3 feet (1 meter) high. Others are medium size, with pitchers about 6 inches (15 centimeters) high. All eat spiders and crickets, wasps, and other insects careless enough to wander into the pitcher trap.

There are eight different types of pitcher plants. The most common is *Sarracenia purpurea*. The common pitcher plant looks more like a red, green, or purple vase than a pitcher. Special cells all over the outer pitcher leaf make a sugary nectar. There is extra nectar at the pitcher top. This isn't by plant accident. It's another way of outsmarting an insect.

A sweet-loving gnat lands on the brightly colored pitcher top. A beetle starts at plant bot-

PITFALL TRAPS: NORTH AMERICAN PITCHER PLANTS

Downward-pointing hairs guide a beetle into the throat of a pitcher.

tom, then crawls greedily upward. But once the beetle and gnat start down the pitcher's shiny waxy inner surface, they are caught. The inner rim of the pitcher, so wet with nectar, is not only slippery but also contains many smooth downward-pointing hairs. It's like being on a slide. There's no way to stop until the insects reach bottom.

The insects try to crawl out. But above the water line is another ring of downward-pointing bristles. Insects can't get over this barrier. Each time they try, they fall back into the water. Soon they stop moving.

20

Now digestive juices go to work, creating a murky insect soup. The pitcher's walls absorb the nutrients, which travel through the plant.

Leftover shells pile up in the bottom of the pitcher. By the end of summer, there is often quite a tidy garbage heap. One large pitcher can have the remains of thousands of dead insects in it at once.

The shells of digested insects have piled up inside this pitcher.

Can you see how the cobra plant got its name?

The cobra plant (*Darlingtonia californica*) has pitchers resembling yellow-green snakes ready to strike. These pitchers grow from 4 to 30 inches (10 to 75 centimeters) tall. The top of a pitcher curves almost completely over a round opening, like a hood. A long divided flap dangles from the front edge of the opening. This flap resembles a snake's tongue or fangs. The "tongue" is covered with glands that produce a sweet-smelling nectar. Sometimes the nectar is so plentiful, it drips down onto the ground. Nectar covers the outside of the pitcher, too.

COBRA PLANTS

Up toward the top of the pitcher crawls an ant, or many ants. Most of the nectar is up there. But there are also hairs at the top, pointing downward into the pitcher. Climbing the tongue takes the ants directly to the pitcher's opening. They reach the top, ready for a meal.

The ants begin feeding under the hood. There, among the dark greens of the leaf, are lighter areas. Like windows, they let sunlight into the plant. Many insects don't like entering dark places from which it seems they can't escape. But

23

Looking up into the cobra hood, an insect would be attracted to the "window" and find itself trapped.

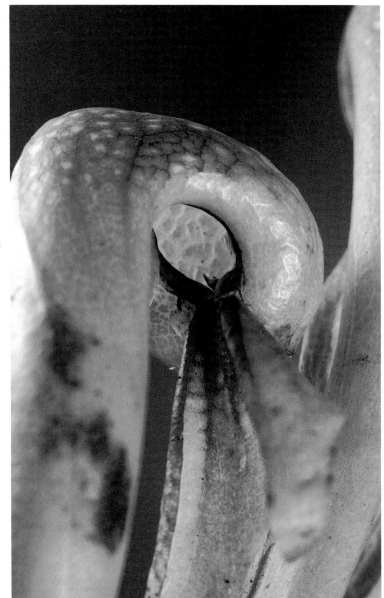

the light from the cobra pitcher "windows" fools them into thinking there are many ways to get out. The ants try to crawl out one window, then another. It isn't too long before they slip on the smooth sides of the cobra pitcher, falling into the water at the bottom. Some try to crawl out, but there are more downward-pointing hairs above the water zone. These hairs make the water a prison.

Unlike the other pitcher plants, the cobra doesn't have digestive *enzymes*. Its meals are broken down by bacteria living in the water. Soon there's nothing left of the ants but skeletons. The rest has been made into a soup that is absorbed by the pitcher.

A butterwort has pretty flowers, but its leaves are deadly traps for small insects.

If you stroke a butterwort, it feels like melted butter over fuzz. This yellow-green carnivorous plant's Latin name is *Pinguicula,* from the Latin word "pinguis," meaning fat. There are at least thirty different kinds of butterworts. The most common one is *Pinguicula vulgaris.*

Sniff a butterwort and it may smell cheesy or musty. This smell convinces a passing insect that the plant has protein-type food. But two types of fluids cover the butterwort's fuzzy

THE BUTTERWORTS

leaves. Both are produced by special glands. One fluid is gluelike. And the other has enzymes that make soup out of any tiny insect that lands in the glue.

When a tiny mayfly lands on the butterwort, it gets stuck. The mayfly's struggles start *digestive* juices flowing. Meanwhile, the leaf edges roll inward. The curled leaf holds these juices like a bowl, and the mayfly soon suffocates.

The mayfly is dissolved into small parts, to be absorbed by glands on the butterwort's surface. In a few days, the leaf uncurls. All that is left of the mayfly are a few pieces of shell.

Insect remains, bits of leaves
and seeds, and other debris litter
the sticky leaves of a butterwort.

Butterworts also absorb pollen, seed parts, and anything else with food value that lands on the sticky leaves. Butterworts would absorb big insects, too, if their leaves were sticky enough to hold them. But big insects usually manage to get unstuck and crawl away.

When nonfood items get stuck, the butterworts don't give off digestive fluid. How do they know the difference between pollen, seeds, sand, rain, and a curious person's poking? Somehow they do. Perhaps they give anything that lands on them the nitrogen taste test. If something doesn't have nitrogen, it's not food for the plant.

A butterwort leaf curls around an unfortunate insect.

Rosettes of sundew leaves, each with sticky tentacles.

Sundews have insect-trapping juice covering the many reddish hairs on their leaves. These hairs, with rounded heads, are called tentacles. In the sunlight the clear juice shines crystal bright, like dew. If you touch the shiny leaves with your finger, they feel sticky. The scientific name of sundews is *Drosera,* from the Greek word *drosos,* meaning dew. Many people call sundews "flypaper carnivorous plants."

FLYPAPER TRAP: THE SUNDEW

There are about one hundred different sundew species. Smaller ones, some less than ½ inch (about a centimeter) high, trap only small insects. Larger ones, primarily found in Africa and Australia, will reach 3 feet (1 meter) high. These trap small animals, such as mice, as well as insects of all sizes.

Both flying and crawling insects are first attracted to the sundew's glistening leaves. Then the insect, perhaps an aphid, smells the sweet juice. The aphid thinks of a meal. But on landing, its feet get stuck. It wriggles, and its wings get stuck. The more the aphid tries to escape, the more sticky juice the sundew's tentacles make.

31

An aphid has become hopelessly trapped in the tentacles of a sundew leaf.

Tentacles near the struggling insect begin bending over it. The leaf edge may begin curling in, bringing the aphid closer to the large number of tentacles at the leaf center. Soon the insect is covered with a basket of tentacles.

Now glands in the tentacle top begin making digestive juices. In about five days, all that is left of the insect is a hard shell. The tentacles uncurl, ready for another meal.

Since each trapping uses up tentacle energy, the sundew doesn't go after nonfood items, such as pebbles. But if a nitrogen-containing food is placed near the plant, the sundew actually stretches a sticky leaf toward the meal.

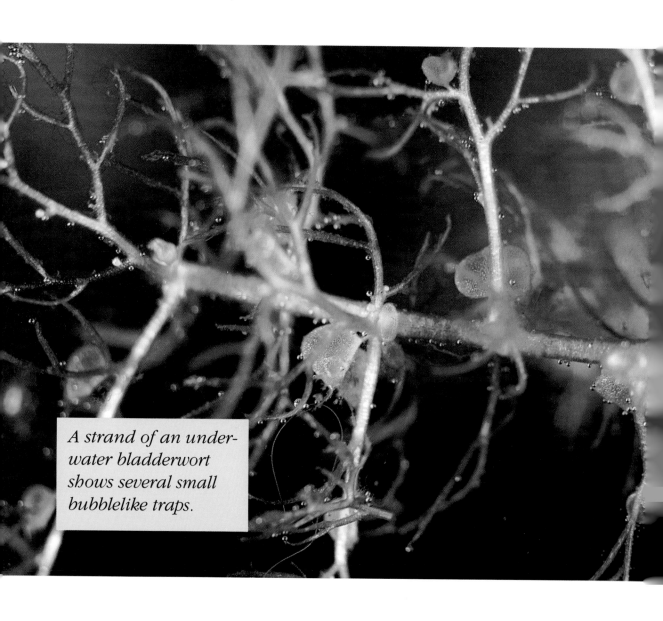

A strand of an under-water bladderwort shows several small bubblelike traps.

Attached to the bladderwort's hairlike green leafstalks are what appear to be many very tiny, partially inflated balloons. These are bladderwort traps. A medium-size bladderwort trap is about the size of this letter "o." A very big trap is about twice the size of the letter "Q."

Bladderworts usually float just below the shallow surface of quiet waters, such as ponds. They have no roots. They look very harmless. But they're not. Each tiny trap is usually quite trigger-happy and waiting for a meal to wander in its direction.

The smallest water creatures, such as rotifers, mosquito larvae, and water fleas, swim by. They may not notice that the little balloon has antennae. The water fleas are looking for food, too, or perhaps a place to hide from fish and other big predators.

The bladderwort trap's antennae create a funnel that leads a tiny creature, perhaps a water flea, toward an invisible closed trapdoor. Gland cells around the door give off a gluelike substance, keeping water out of the bladderwort.

MOUSETRAP PLANTS: THE BLADDERWORTS

35

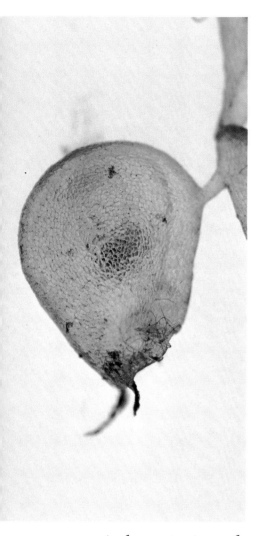

A close-up view of a bladderwort trap.

Other gland cells on the door give off a sugary substance. The water flea moves closer and closer toward the sweet smell.

At the bottom edge of the trapdoor are four pointed bristles. As soon as the water flea touches the bristles, the trapdoor opens inward and the water flea is sucked inside, along with water. The trapdoor slams shut. All this happens in a tiny fraction of a second. The water flea has no chance to escape.

The bladderwort trap is now rounder. It is full of water plus its meal. Slowly, special glands remove water through the trap's walls. But the water flea can't get out. It may swim around for a while. But eventually it dies.

Now special glands release digestive enzymes and acids. The victim becomes smaller and smaller. Soon the glands absorb it, and the nutrients are carried to the rest of the bladderwort. Just twenty minutes later, the bladder is ready to catch another meal. As many as twelve tiny animals can be found in one bladder at the same time.

Bladderworts grow all over the world. Their scientific name is *Utricularia*. Most of the 250 kinds grow in water. But some bladderworts grow in other wet places. For example, one type grows in South America amid decaying leaves on the forest floor. Others grow on moss. But they all bait a trap with sugary material, then whoosh in their hungry, or curious, tiny victims.

Nepenthes *pitchers hang from the trees in the rain forests of Borneo.*

On a very hot day in tropical Borneo, a small rat looks for water in the bottom of a big purple leaf shaped like a fat pitcher. The rat is very thirsty. And the plant doesn't seem dangerous. So the rat sticks its head in the wide opening. Oh, it can't quite reach the water. It sticks its head in a little farther. Now it can drink. The water is dark with dead insects floating about, but it is better than no water at all.

NEPENTHES: TROPICAL PITCHER PLANTS

Satisfied, the rat tries to pull its head out. But there are downward-pointing teeth around the pitcher's opening. The rat can't pull its head out. It crawls in a little farther, trying to get loose. But the more it crawls in, the more of it is stuck. After a while, the rat drowns.

Eventually the rat is dissolved by the pitcher's enzymes. Soon only a few bones remain. As the pitcher gets older, small monkey bones, scorpion parts, and lizard bones join the refuse heap at its bottom. Some of these victims were just curious. Others sought a drink or an easy insect meal. A few were looking for a safe place to hide.

There are about eighty species of tropical pitcher plants, most growing in humid jungles. Few are as large as the Borneo *Nepenthes rajah,* which can have pitchers 14 inches (36 centimeters) long and about half that wide. The more common *Nepenthes mirabilis* has light-green pitchers only 6 inches (15 centimeters) long. The pitchers of other species may be chocolate-brown, dark red, or yellow-green. They grow on vines. Some vines climb to the tops of trees, with pitchers dangling high in the air. Others trail along the ground, their pitchers resting on the soil surface.

Insects are attracted to the sweet-smelling nectar covering the inner part of the brightly colored lid. From here they walk onto the hard, shiny, round leaf rim. The rim is prettily colored in red and green stripes. Each stripe, or rib, ends within the pitcher as a sharp downward-pointing tooth. Between these pretty teeth are more nectar-producing glands.

Insects soon seek out this extra nectar. But right below the ribbed rim is a waxy area. When the insects walk on this, the wax sticks to their feet. The insects can't hold on to the wall of the pitcher anymore. Down they ski into the water. Their struggles help the pitcher secrete digestive enzymes and acid. Sometimes a few insects reach the pitcher sides and try to climb out again. But when they get to the wax layer near the top, they fall right back down into the water.

A fly is digested in two days. A tiny midge is digested within hours.

Many Nepenthes *pitchers have exotic colors and patterns.*

Many insects are victims of the trumpet pitcher plant, but this fly is safe. It even lays its eggs in the pitcher.

Some insects get along so well with certain carnivorous plants that they make their home on them. Certain spiders, assassin bugs, moth caterpillars, and mosquito larvae can live in pitchers. Other insects, such as the *Byblis* bug, can live safely on a sticky leaf.

Look inside some pitchers and you may see a spider web draped across the top. In the web are several struggling insects. They were attracted to sweet-smelling nectar at the pitcher's rim. When they slipped, instead of landing in the water, they landed in the spider's web. The spider has a fine meal. Its leftovers drop into the water, so the pitcher plant gets its share of food. Why doesn't the spider slip down the pitcher's sides to become a meal itself? It uses its web as a safety net.

Sarcophaga flies can also live in some pitcher plants. The female fly lays eggs on the upper inner part of the pitcher. When the young hatch, they fall into the liquid. But instead of drowning or becoming pitcher food, they begin feeding on dead insects. A special substance on their bodies

INSECTS THAT LIKE CARNIVOROUS PLANTS

43

A small frog has found a perfect hiding place in this Venezuelan pitcher plant.

protects them from the pitcher's digestive enzymes. When the fly maggots reach full size, they chew a hole in the pitcher wall, crawl out, and *pupate* on the ground near the pitcher. Soon a new fly emerges, and the cycle starts again.

There's even a wasp that makes its home in pitcher plants. The *Sarracenia* wasp first stuffs the pitcher pool with grass. On top of this, the wasp makes layers of freshly killed grasshoppers and crickets, separating each layer with more grass. Then it lays eggs among the dead insects, covering this with a layer of grass. The pitcher plant has become a wasp nest.

And once in a while, if you peek inside a pitcher plant, you may see a small tree frog peeking back at you. The frog knows that insects come to the pitchers looking for food. The tree frog clings to the slippery walls of the pitcher with the suction pads on its feet and gets many easy meals. But every so often a frog is careless and slips—and the pitcher plant gets an easy meal.

Carnivorous plants such as these Malaysian pitchers grow plentifully when conditions are right.

Carnivorous plants still grow plentifully where people do not invade their living space. But they are delicate. They don't like changes in their living conditions.

All types of *contamination* will kill carnivorous plants, including pesticides, fertilizers, sewage, and industrial waste. When housing developments, shopping centers, and factories are built, they alter land that was once used by carnivorous plants. Construction and other projects may change land slope and water flow or drain the water altogether.

CARNIVOROUS PLANT SURVIVAL

Sometimes even people who mean well help destroy pitcher plants. Flower arrangers clip the unusual-looking leaves. Without leaves, the carnivorous plant cannot make food. It will starve.

Collectors can become so excited about a beautiful carnivorous plant that they carry it away. But each plant makes the seeds for future plants. Take the plant away, and no plants may replace it. That particular type of carnivorous plant could die out, or become extinct.

A Venus flytrap has caught a cricket. In North Carolina, where this plant grows, and in many other areas, these plants are in danger of dying out.

While quite a few carnivorous plants can be raised in home terrariums, most plants taken from the wild won't survive. Never take plants from the wild or buy them from someone who collects them in the wild. Buy only nursery-raised plants. Ask when you buy them.

If you are interested in growing carnivorous plants, you may find them in some plant stores. You will have to look up these stores in the telephone book and ask if they have carnivorous plants.

This tropical pitcher plant grows well in a container, but it needs the warmth and dampness of a greenhouse to thrive.

Each carnivorous plant type is different and has somewhat different growing requirements. But there are general rules to follow.

Where to Grow: A sunny windowsill is the easiest place for beginners to grow carnivorous plants. As you acquire more plants, you may want to obtain a terrarium (an uncovered fish tank will do).

Containers: Square plastic pots work well because you can put several next to each other. This helps keep up the humidity, or moisture level, around the plants. Wash the pots before you use them. All the pots should have a small drainage hole.

Place all pots in plastic trays that will hold water. If you purchase a potted plant with a plastic cover, remove the cover so the plant can trap insects.

Soil: If you purchase your plant from a good nursery, you probably won't have to change the soil until the plant gets too large for the pot. Always purchase soil. Never use garden soil, as it may contain materials harmful to carnivorous plants. These plants do well in combinations of

GROWING CARNIVOROUS PLANTS

granulated moss peat, garden nursery sand, and perlite. Do not use builder's sand, beach sand, sedge peat, or any peat containing fertilizer. The following are very basic soil guidelines.

Venus flytrap:
one part peat to one part sand

Sundew:
two parts peat to one part sand

Trumpet pitcher:
six parts peat, two parts perlite, one part sand

Water: Keep about an inch of water in the plastic tray surrounding the pot. The soil should remain wet at all times, but not soggy. Water should soak up into the planting pot from the bottom tray. Do not put water on the leaves.

Use distilled or deionized water, which you can buy in bottles at most supermarkets. Rainwater is also good, although in some areas it can contain impurities from the air. Always collect rainwater in a very clean plastic container, and keep it in a clean plastic container with a lid. Never use water from the faucet or from home water softeners. It may contain chemicals that are harmful to carnivorous plants.

Fertilizer: Do not fertilize carnivorous plants. They grow naturally in poor soil. Fertilizer causes root rot and will soon kill your plant.

Insect Food: It is best to let your plants trap their own food. If you keep your plants on a windowsill, and some flies or other insects enter the room from time to time, the plants will attract and trap them on their own.

If you are growing carnivorous plants in a classroom or other place where insects don't normally enter, the teacher may allow a student to catch a fly or two each week and leave them flying in the room overnight. They will be attracted to the plants and become a meal.

Do not feed your plants dead insects. And never feed them raw hamburger or other raw meat. This will cause the traps to rot.

You may be tempted to experiment with different foods and liquids. But this will almost certainly harm your carnivorous plants. It is more fun to succeed at growing healthy plants.

Winter Care: Like many other plants, carnivorous plants rest in winter. Sometimes the plant just stops growing. Other times leaves dry and die back. If this happens to your plant, give it less water, so that the soil is just damp rather than saturated. Keep it in filtered sunlight instead of direct sun. It should begin to grow again in the spring.

Botanical. Relating to plants.

Chlorophyll. The green coloring matter of plants and leaves that helps change the sun's light energy into chemical energy.

Contamination. Impurities added by contact or mixture.

Digestive juices. Fluids that change food or drink into a form absorbable by the organism.

Enzymes. The proteins that promote chemical change.

Gland. An organ, made up of many cells or just a single cell, whose main function is to build up specific chemical compounds that are passed to the outside of the gland.

Nectar. A sweet fluid within a flower that attracts insects.

Nutrients. Minerals and vitamins that are vital building blocks for the cells that make up any organism.

Peat. Partially decayed plant material found in swamps.

GLOSSARY

Pollen. Powdery yellow grains produced in the male part of a plant.

Pupate. To change from a larval, or immature, insect to an adult form.

Skeleton. The hard supporting or covering part of an organism.

Wetland. An area where the ground is saturated or soaked with water.

FIND OUT MORE ABOUT INSECT-EATING PLANTS

People who study and enjoy raising carnivorous plants are often members of the International Carnivorous Plant Society (ICPS). Young people are welcome. For information, write to:

ICPS
Fullerton Arboretum
California State University
Fullerton, CA 92634

Enclose a self-addressed stamped envelope. (The society is staffed by volunteers, so there may be a short wait for a reply.) ICPS has a membership fee. The organization sponsors both carnivorous-plant shows and educational forums, and members receive a regular magazine. The magazine lists places where you can buy seed and nursery-grown plants, as well as special botanical collections where you can see carnivorous plants. Some local ICPS chapters have meetings, slide shows, and plant sales.

For detailed information on how to grow carnivorous plants, consult the ICPS bulletin or a book such as *Insect-Eating Plants and How To Grow Them* by Adrian Slack (University of Washington Press, 1986). Check your library for other books about these fascinating plants.

Carnivorous plants being grown at California State University, Fullerton.

Page numbers in *italics* refer
to illustrations.

INDEX

A member of the International Carnivorous Plant Society, L. Patricia Kite has written about such fascinating creatures as sea slugs, jellyfish, and crabs in her previous books for young readers. She holds a teaching credential in biology and a master's degree in journalism, and her articles on carnivorous plants have appeared in *Flower & Garden* and other publications. She lives in Newark, California.

ABOUT THE AUTHOR